CLASSIC STARTS™

The Wind in the Willows

Retold from the Kenneth Grahame original by Martin Woodside

Illustrated by Jamel Akib

STERLING

New York / London
www.sterlingpublishing.com/kids

STERLING and the distinctive Sterling logo are registered trademarks of
Sterling Publishing Co., Inc.

Library of Congress Cataloging-in-Publication Data

Woodside, Martin.
 The wind in the willows / retold from the Kenneth Grahame original by
Martin Woodside ; illustrated by Jamel Akib ; afterword by Arthur Pober, EdD.
    p. cm.—(Classic starts)
 Summary: An abridged version of Kenneth Grahame's classic tale of the
escapades of four animal friends who live along a river in the English country-
side—Toad, Mole, Rat, and Badger.
 ISBN 978-1-4027-3696-4
 [1. Animals—Fiction.] I. Akib, Jamel, ill. II. Grahame, Kenneth, 1859–1932.
Wind in the willows. III. Title. IV. Series.

PZ7.W867Win 2007
[Fic]—dc22

                                                          2006014669

Lot#:
8 10 9
05/15

Published by Sterling Publishing Co., Inc.
387 Park Avenue South, New York, NY 10016
Copyright © 2007 by Martin Woodside
Illustrations copyright © 2007 by Jamel Akib
Distributed in Canada by Sterling Publishing
c/o Canadian Manda Group, 165 Dufferin Street,
Toronto, Ontario, Canada M6K 3H6
Distributed in the United Kingdom by GMC Distribution Services,
Castle Place, 166 High Street, Lewes, East Sussex, England BN7 1XU
Distributed in Australia by Capricorn Link (Australia) Pty. Ltd.
P.O. Box 704, Windsor, NSW 2756, Australia

Classic Starts is a trademark of Sterling Publishing Co., Inc.

Printed in China
All rights reserved

Sterling ISBN 978-1-4027-3696-4

For information about custom editions, special sales, premium and
corporate purchases, please contact Sterling Special Sales
Department at 800-805-5489 or specialsales@sterlingpublishing.com.

CONTENTS

CHAPTER 1

The Riverbank

❧

The Mole had been working very hard all the morning, spring cleaning. First with brooms, then with dusters, then on ladders and steps and chairs, till he had dust in his throat and eyes, and an aching back and weary arms.

Spring was moving in the air above and in the air below and around him, even his dark and lowly little house. It was small wonder, then, that he suddenly flung down his brush on the floor, said "No more spring cleaning!" and bolted out of the house without even waiting to put on his coat.

Something above was calling him. So he scraped and scraped and scratched and scraped, working busily with his little paws and muttering, "Up we go, up we go," till at last, pop! His snout came out into the sunlight, and he found himself rolling in the warm grass of a green meadow.

The sunshine struck hot on his fur and soft breezes soothed his heated brow. He rambled busily through the meadows. Birds were building nests, flowers were budding—everything was happy. His happiness was complete when suddenly he stood by the edge of a river. He had never seen a river before. It was chasing and chuckling, gripping things with a gurgle and leaving them with a laugh. The Mole was delighted. He sat on the bank while the river chattered to him. It was the finest sound he had ever heard.

A dark hole in the riverbank opposite caught his eye. As he gazed, something bright and small seemed to twinkle in the heart of it like a tiny star.

Then as he looked, it winked at him. It was an eye! A small face gradually began to grow around it.

A little brown face, with whiskers.

It had small neat ears and thick silky hair.

It was the Water Rat!

"Hello, Mole!" said the Water Rat.

"Hello, Rat!" said the Mole.

The Rat stepped onto a little boat that Mole had not observed. It was painted blue outside, and white within, and was just the size for two animals. Mole's whole heart went out to it at once. The Rat rowed across smartly. Then he held up his forepaw as the Mole stepped gingerly down. "Lean on that!" he said. "Now then, step lively!" And the Mole, to his surprise, found himself seated in a real boat.

"This has been a wonderful day," said he, as the Rat shoved off. "Do you know, I've never been in a boat before."

"What?" cried the Rat, openmouthed. "Never

been—you never—well, I—what have you been doing then?"

"Is it so nice as all that?" asked the Mole shyly.

"Nice? It's the *only* thing," said the Water Rat dreamily. "Believe me, my young friend, there is *nothing*—absolutely nothing—half so much fun as being in a boat."

Absorbed in his new life, in the sparkle, the ripple, the scents, the sounds, and the sunlight, the Mole trailed a paw in the water and day-dreamed.

"I beg your pardon," said the Mole, pulling himself together with an effort. "You must think me very rude, but all this is so new to me. So, this is a river?"

"*The* river," corrected the Rat

"And you really live by the river? What a jolly life! What lies over *there*?" asked the Mole, waving a paw toward a background of dark trees on one side of the river.

"That's just the Wild Wood," said the Rat shortly. "We don't go there very much, we river-bankers."

"Aren't they—aren't they very *nice* people in there?" said the Mole, a bit nervously.

"W-ell," replied the Rat, "let me see. The squirrels are all right, but the rabbits are a mixed lot. And then there's Badger, of course. Nobody interferes with *him*. They had better not," he said significantly.

"And, of course—there are others," continued the Rat in a hesitating sort of way. "Weasels— and stoats—and foxes—and so on. They're all right in a way—but there's no denying it— well—you can't really trust them and that's the fact."

The Mole knew well that an animal with good manners does not dwell on possible trouble ahead, so he dropped the subject.

"And beyond the Wild Wood?" the Mole

asked. "It looks all blue and dim, and one sees what may be hills and something like the smoke of towns, or is only a cloud drift?"

"Beyond the Wild Wood comes the Human World," said the Rat, "and that's something that doesn't matter, either to you or to me. I've never been there and I'm never going, nor you, either, if you've got any sense. Now then! We're going to lunch."

The Rat brought the boat alongside the bank, tied it up, helped awkward Mole safely ashore, and swung out the picnic basket. The Mole begged to be allowed to unpack it all by himself. He took out all the mysterious packets one by one and arranged their contents, gasping "O my! O my!" at each fresh surprise. When all was ready, the Rat said, "Now dig in, old fellow!" and the Mole was very glad to obey, for he had started his spring cleaning at a very early hour and was now quite hungry.

CHAPTER 2

New Friends and a New Life

⌒℘

"What are you looking at?" said the Rat, when the edge of their hunger was somewhat dulled.

"I am looking," said the Mole, "at a streak of bubbles that I see traveling along the surface of the water."

Suddenly, a flat glistening nose showed itself above the edge of the bank, and the Otter pulled himself out and shook the water from his coat.

"How greedy!" he cried. "Why didn't you invite me, Ratty?"

"This was an unplanned lunch," explained the Rat. "By the way—meet my friend Mr. Mole."

"Proud, I'm sure," said the Otter, and the two animals were friends.

There was a rustle behind them coming from a hedge where last year's leaves still clung thick. A stripy head, with high shoulders behind it, popped out.

"Come on, old Badger!" shouted the Rat.

The Badger trotted forward a pace or two, then grunted, "H'm! Company," and turned his back and disappeared from view.

"That's just the sort of fellow he is!" observed Rat. "He simply hates society! Well, tell us, who's out on the river?"

"Toad's out, for one," replied the Otter. "In his brand-new racing boat, new clothes, new everything!"

Otter and Rat looked at each other and laughed.

"Once it was nothing but sailing," said the Rat. "Then he tired of that and took to racing. Whatever he takes up, he gets tired of it, and starts something fresh."

"Such a good fellow, too," remarked the Otter. "But no stability—especially in a boat. Did I ever tell you the story about Toad and that time when he—"

But no one heard the end of the story that day. Just then, a fly swerved unsteadily above the river. There was a swirl of water, and a "cloop," and the fly was gone. So was Otter.

The Mole looked down. There was a streak of bubbles on the surface of the water.

The Rat hummed a tune, and Mole remembered that animal manners forbid any sort of comment on the sudden disappearance of one's friends at any moment.

The afternoon sun was getting low as the Rat rowed gently homeward in a dreamy mood, murmuring poetry over to himself, and not paying much attention to Mole. But the Mole was very full of lunch and self-satisfaction and already quite at home in a boat (so he thought). He was getting a bit restless besides, and soon said, "Ratty! Please, *I* want to row, now!"

The Rat shook his head, with a smile. "Not yet, my young friend," he said. "Wait till you've had a few lessons. It's not as easy as it looks."

The Mole was quiet for a minute or two. But he began to feel more and more jealous of Rat, rowing so strongly and so easily along. His pride began to whisper that he could do it every bit as well. He jumped up and seized the oars so suddenly that the Rat, who was gazing out over water, was taken by surprise and fell backward off his seat with his legs in the air.

"Stop it, you *silly* fool!" cried the Rat, from the bottom of the boat. "You can't do it! You'll tip us over!"

The Mole flung his oars back with a flourish, and made a great dig at the water. He missed the surface altogether, his legs flew up above his head, and he found himself lying on top of the Rat. Greatly alarmed, he made a grab at the side of the boat, and the next moment—sploosh!

Over went the boat, and the Mole found himself struggling in the river.

O my, how cold the water was, and O how *very* wet it felt. How it sang in his ears as he went down, down, down! Then a firm paw gripped him by the back of his neck. It was the Rat, and he was laughing—at least the Mole could *feel* him laughing, right down his arm and through his paw, and into Mole's neck.

The Rat got hold of an oar and shoved it under the Mole's arm. Then he did the same by the other side of him and, swimming behind, propelled the helpless animal to shore. He hauled

him out and set him down on the bank, a squashy
lump of misery.

So the dismal Mole, wet without and ashamed
within, trotted about the bank till he was fairly
dry. The Rat plunged into the water again, recov-
ered the boat and turned it over, and dived successfully for the picnic basket.

When they were ready to go again, Mole, limp
and dejected, took his seat in the stern of the boat
and said in a low voice, broken with emotion,
"Ratty, my generous friend! I am very sorry for
my foolish and ungrateful conduct."

"That's all right," responded the Rat cheerily.
"What's a little wet to a Water Rat? Don't you
think any more about it. And look here, I really
think you had better come and stop with me for a
little time. I'll teach you to row and to swim, and
you'll soon be as handy on the water as any of us."

When they got home, the Rat made a bright

fire in the parlor, and planted the Mole in an armchair in front of it. He fetched down a dressing gown and slippers for him, and told him river stories till suppertime. Very thrilling stories they were, too, to an earth-dwelling animal such as Mole.

This day was only the first of many similar ones for the Mole. He came to live with the Rat for a while. There he learned to swim and to row and to listen to the wind whispering in the reeds. He came to know the joy of the river.

CHAPTER 3

The Open Road

ᥱᡢ

"Ratty," said the Mole suddenly, one bright summer morning, "I want to ask you a favor."

The Rat was sitting on the riverbank, singing a little song. Since the early morning, he had been swimming in the river in company with his friends the ducks.

"What I wanted to ask you was, won't you take me to call on Mr. Toad? I've heard so much about him, and I do so want to meet him."

"Why, certainly," said the good-natured Rat, jumping to his feet. "Get the boat out, and we'll paddle up there at once. It's never the wrong time to call on Toad. Always good-tempered, always glad to see you, always sorry when you go!"

"He must be a very nice animal," observed the Mole, as he got into the boat and took the oars. Rat settled himself comfortably in the stern.

"He is indeed the best of animals," replied Rat. "Perhaps he's not very clever, and it may be that he is both boastful and conceited, but Toady has got some great qualities."

Rounding a bend in the river, they came in sight of a handsome, dignified old house of mellowed red brick, with well-kept lawns reaching down to the water's edge.

"There's Toad Hall," said the Rat. "And that creek on the left, where the notice board says PRIVATE. NO LANDING ALLOWED, leads to the boathouse where we'll leave the boat. The stables are over there to the right. That's the banquet hall you're looking at now—very old that is. Toad is rather rich, you know, and this is really one of the nicest houses in these parts, though we never admit as much to Toad."

They glided up the creek and passed into the shadow of a large boathouse. Here they saw many beautiful boats, slung from the cross-beams or

hauled up on a slip, but none in the water. The Rat looked around. "I wonder what new fad he has taken up now? We shall hear all about it quite soon enough."

They strolled across the lawns in search of Toad, whom they presently happened upon resting in a garden chair with a large map spread out on his knees.

"Hooray!" he cried, jumping up on seeing them. "This is splendid!" He shook the paws of both of them warmly, never waiting for an introduction to Mole. "I was just going to send a boat down the river for you, Ratty. You don't know how lucky it is, your turning up just now!"

"Let's sit quiet a bit, Toady!" said the Rat, throwing himself into an easy chair, while the Mole took another by the side of him.

"Now, look there," Toad said. "You've got to help me. It's most important."

"It's about your rowing, I suppose," said the

Rat with an innocent air. "With a great deal of patience, and some expert coaching, you may—"

"O, pooh! Boating!" interrupted the Toad, in great disgust. "I've given that up *long* ago. Sheer waste of time, that's what it is. No, I've discovered the real thing, the only true occupation for a lifetime. Come with me, dear Ratty, and your friend also, if he will be so very good, just as far as the stable yard."

He led the way to the stable yard accordingly, the Rat following with a most distrustful expression. There, in front of the coach house, they saw a shiny and new horse-drawn carriage. It had red wheels and was painted canary yellow with a green trim.

"There you are!" cried the Toad. "There's real life for you. The open road, the dusty highway. The whole world before you and a horizon that's always changing! And mind, this is the finest cart of its sort that was ever built. Come inside and look at the details. Planned 'em all myself, I did!"

It was indeed very compact and comfortable. Little sleeping bunks, a little table that folded up against a wall, a cooking stove, lockers, book-shelves, a birdcage with a bird in it, and pots, pans, jugs, and kettles of every size and variety.

"All complete!" said the Toad triumphantly. "You'll find that nothing has been forgotten when we make our start this afternoon."

"I beg your pardon," said the Rat slowly, as he chewed a straw, "but did I overhear you say something about *we* and *start* and *this afternoon*?"

"Now, you dear old good Ratty," said Toad, "don't begin talking in that stiff and sniffy kind of way. I want to show you the whole world! I'm going to make an animal of you, my boy!"

"I don't care," said the Rat stubbornly, quite displeased with Toad's sudden change of heart toward boating. "I'm not coming and that's flat.

And what's more, Mole's going to stick by me, aren't you, Mole?"

"Of course I am" said the Mole loyally. "I'll always stick with you, Rat. But it sounds as if it might have been—well, rather fun, you know!"

The Rat saw what was passing in his mind, and wavered. He hated disappointing people, and he was fond of Mole, and would do almost anything to make him happy.

Toad was watching both of them very closely. "Come along in and have some lunch," he said diplomatically, "and we'll talk it over. I only want to give pleasure to you fellows. 'Live for others!' That's my motto in life."

During lunch, which was excellent, of course—everything at Toad Hall always was—Toad painted the prospects of the trip and the joys of the open life and the roadside in such glowing colors that the Mole could hardly sit in his chair for excitement. The Rat, though still unconvinced, allowed his good nature to override his personal objections. He could not bear to disappoint his two friends, who were already planning out each day's adventures for several weeks ahead.

CHAPTER 4

The Motorcar's Spell

⁓

Once the horse was harnessed, they set off, all talking at once. It was a golden afternoon. The smell of the dust they kicked up was rich and satisfying. Out of thick orchards on either side of them, birds whistled to them cheerily, and rabbits, sitting at their front doors in the bushes, held up their forepaws and said, "O my! O my! O my!"

Late in the evening, tired and happy, they drew up to a remote field, turned the horse loose to graze, and ate their simple supper sitting on the grass. Toad talked about all he was going to do in the days to come, while stars grew fuller and larger all around them. A yellow moon, appearing suddenly and silently from nowhere in particular, came to keep them company and listen to their talk. At last, they turned into their little bunks in the cart.

After so much open air and excitement the Toad slept very soundly, and no amount of shaking could rouse him out of bed next morning. So the Rat saw to the horse and lit a fire while the Mole trudged off to the nearest village for milk and eggs, which the Toad had, of course, forgotten. The hard work had all been done, and the two animals were resting by the time Toad appeared on the scene, fresh and relaxed. He remarked what a pleasant, easy life it was they were all leading now, after leaving the cares and worries and fatigues of housekeeping at home.

They had a pleasant ramble that day. It was not until afternoon that they came out on the high road, and there disaster sprang out on them. They were strolling along easily. The Mole was by the horse's head, talking to him, since the horse had complained that he was being frightfully left out of it. The Toad and the Water Rat were walking behind the cart talking together when far behind them they heard a faint warning hum, like the drone of a distant bee. Glancing back, they saw a cloud of dust with a dark center of energy. It was advancing on them at incredible speed, while from the dust a faint "poop-poop!" sound wailed like an uneasy animal in pain.

In an instant, the peaceful scene was changed. The "poop-poop" sound rang with a brazen shout in their ears. They had a moment's glimpse of a piece of glittering plate glass, and a magnificent motorcar, its driver tense and hugging his wheel, blinded them with a cloud of dust and then dwindled to a speck in the far distance.

The old gray horse, dreaming as he plodded

along, simply abandoned himself to his natural emotions. Rearing, plunging, backing steadily, he drove the cart backward toward the deep ditch at the side of the road. There was a terrible crash— and the canary-colored cart lay on its side in the ditch.

The Rat danced up and down in the road in anger. "You villains!" he shouted, shaking both fists. "You scoundrels, you—you road hogs! I'll have the law after you! I'll report you! I'll take you through the courts!"

Toad sat straight down in the middle of the dusty road, his legs stretched out before him, and stared in the direction of the disappearing motor-car. His breath was short, his face wore a satisfied expression, and at intervals he faintly murmured, "Poop-poop."

The Mole was busy trying to quiet the horse, which he succeeded in doing after a time. Then he went to look at the cart, on its side in the ditch.

It was indeed a sorry sight: windows smashed, axles hopelessly bent, one wheel off, and sardine tins scattered.

The Rat came to help him, but even together they could not lift up the cart. "Hey, Toad!" they cried. "Come and lend a hand!"

The Toad didn't answer or budge from his seat in the road. Rat and Mole found him in a sort of trance, a happy smile on his face, his eyes still fixed on the dusty trail of their destroyer. He was still heard to whisper, "Poop-poop."

"What are we to do with him?" asked the Mole of the Water Rat.

"Nothing at all," replied the Rat firmly. "He has got a new craze, and it always takes him this way, in its first stage. He'll continue like that for days now, like an animal walking in a happy dream. He will be quite useless for practical purposes. Never mind him."

The Rat knotted the horse's reins over his

back and took him by the head, carrying the bird-cage that had fallen from the cart in his other hand. "Come on!" he said grimly to the Mole. "It's five or six miles to the nearest town, and we shall just have to walk."

They had not gone very far on their way, however, when there was a pattering of feet behind them, and Toad caught up and thrust a paw inside the elbow of each of them.

"Now look here, Toad!" said the Rat sharply. "As soon as we get to the town, you'll have to go to the police station and lodge a complaint against it. And then you'll have to arrange for the cart to be picked up and fixed."

"Police station! Complaint!" murmured Toad dreamily. "Me *complain* of that beautiful, that heavenly vision! *Fix the cart!* I'm done with carts forever. O Ratty! You can't think how thankful I am to you for coming on this trip! I wouldn't have gone without you, and I might never have seen that swan, that sunbeam, that thunderbolt!"

The Rat turned from him in despair. "You see?" he said to the Mole, addressing him across Toad's head "He's quite hopeless. I give it up—when we get to town we'll go to the railway station, and with any luck we may pick up a train that will get us back to River Bank tonight. And if you ever catch me going along with this crazy animal again!"—he snorted.

The following evening, Mole was sitting on the bank fishing when the Rat came strolling along to find him. "Heard the news?" he said. "There's nothing else being talked about, all along the riverbank. Toad went up to town on an early train this morning. He has ordered a very large and very expensive motorcar."

CHAPTER 5

The Wild Wood

ᥱᢁ

The Mole had long wanted to meet the Badger. But whenever he mentioned his wish to the Water Rat, he always found himself put off. "It's all right," the Rat would say. "Badger will turn up someday or other and then I'll introduce you. The best of fellows! But you must take him not only *as* you find him, but *when* you find him."

"Couldn't you ask him for dinner or something?" said the Mole.

"He wouldn't come," replied the Rat simply. "Badger hates society, and invitations, and dinner, and all that sort of thing."

"Well, then supposing we go and call on *him*," suggested the Mole.

"O, I'm sure he wouldn't like that at *all*," said the Rat, quite alarmed. "He'd be quite offended. Besides, he lives in the very middle of the Wild Wood."

"Well," said the Mole, "you told me the Wild Wood was all right, you know."

"O, I know," the Rat said, trying to avoid the subject. "But it's a long way, and he wouldn't be home at this time of year anyhow. He'll be coming along someday, if you'll wait quietly."

The Mole had to be content with this. And it was not till summer was long over, and the cold and frost kept them indoors, and the swollen river raced past outside their windows, that he found his thoughts once again drifting toward old Badger.

In the wintertime, the Mole had a great deal of spare time on his hands. And so one afternoon, when the Rat was dozing in his armchair before the blaze, he decided to go out by himself and explore the Wild Wood, and perhaps look in on Mr. Badger.

It was a cold still afternoon with a steely sky overhead when he slipped out of the warm parlor into the open air. The country lay bare and entirely leafless around him. All the hidden places that had been mysterious in leafy summer were now exposed. Mole liked the country like this: undecorated, hard, and stripped of its finery. With great cheerfulness he pushed on toward the Wild Wood, which lay before him low and threatening, like a black reef in a deep southern sea.

There was nothing to alarm him at first entry. Twigs cracked under his feet, logs tripped him, but he moved farther into the woods, to where the light was less. The trees crouched nearer and nearer, and holes in their trunks made ugly mouths at him on either side.

Everything was still now. The dusk advanced

on him steadily, rapidly, gathering in behind and ahead. The light seemed to be draining away.

Then the faces began.

It was over his shoulder that he first thought he saw a face: a little wedge-shaped face, looking at him from a hole. When he turned, the thing had vanished.

He passed another hole, and another, and another; and then—yes!—no!—yes!—certainly a little narrow face with hard eyes had flashed up for an instant from a hole, and was gone. He hesitated—and walked on. Then suddenly, every hole, far and near, and there were hundreds of them, seemed to possess its own face, coming and going rapidly, all hard-eyed and evil and sharp.

Then the whistling began.

Very faint and shrill it was, and far behind him, when he first heard it; but somehow it made him hurry forward. Then, still very faint and shrill, it sounded far ahead of him. Mole didn't know which way to turn, and soon the sound broke out on either side of him. They were up and alert and ready, whoever they were! Mole was far from any help, and the night was closing in.

Then the pattering began.

He thought it was only falling leaves at first, so soft and delicate was the sound of it. Then as it grew, he knew it was the pat-pat-pat of little feet. Was it in front or behind? It grew and then it multiplied as he listened in fear, leaning this way and that. It seemed to be closing in on him.

The whole wood seemed to be running now, running hard, hunting, chasing, closing in around something or—somebody? In panic, Mole began to run, too. He ran up against things and he fell over things and into things. It was quite dark now. At last he took refuge in the deep hollow of an old beech tree. As he lay there panting and trembling, he listened to the whistlings and patterings outside. He now knew the terror of the Wild Wood!

CHAPTER 6

Rescued

Meanwhile, the Rat, warm and comfortable, dozed by his fireside. Then a coal slipped, the fire crackled and sent up a spurt of flame, and he woke with a start. He looked around for the Mole.

But the Mole was not there.

He listened for a time. The house seemed very quiet.

Then he called, "Moly!" several times. When he received no answers, he got up and went out into the hall. The Mole's cap was missing from its usual peg. His boots, which always lay by the umbrella stand, were also gone.

The Rat left the house and carefully examined the muddy ground outside, hoping to find the Mole's tracks. There they were, sure enough. The imprints of the boots in the mud led directly to the Wild Wood.

The Rat stood deep in thought for a minute or two, and then set off for the Wild Wood. It was already toward dusk when he reached the first fringe of trees, and he plunged in without hesitation. Here and there, wicked little faces popped out of the holes. He made his way fearlessly through the forest, looking around and calling out cheerfully, "Moly! Moly! Moly! Where are you? It's me—it's old Rat!"

He had hunted through the wood for an hour or more when he heard a little cry answering him. Following the sound, he made his way through the gathering darkness to the foot of an old beech tree with a hole in it, and from out of the hole came a feeble voice saying, "Ratty! Is that really you?"

The Rat crept into the hollow, and there he found the Mole, tired and still trembling. "O Rat!" he cried, "I've been so scared, you can't think!"

"O, I quite understand," said the Rat soothingly. "You shouldn't really have gone and done it, Mole. I did my best to keep you from it. We river-bankers hardly ever come here by ourselves."

The Mole was greatly cheered by the sound of the Rat's voice, and he stopped shivering and began to feel bolder and more himself again.

"Now then," said the Rat presently, "we really must pull ourselves together and make a start for home while there's still light left. It will never do to spend the night here, you understand. For one thing, it will be too cold."

"Dear Ratty," said the poor Mole. "I'm dreadfully sorry, but I'm so tired. You *must* let me rest here awhile longer, and get my strength back."

"O, all right," said the good-natured Rat. "It's pretty nearly pitch dark now, anyhow, and there will be a bit of moon later."

So the Mole stretched himself out and soon dropped off into sleep, though it was a broken and troubled sort of sleep. Rat covered himself up, too, as best he could for warmth, and lay patiently.

When at last the Mole woke up, the Rat said, "Now then, I'll just take a look outside, and if everything's quiet, then we really must be off." He went to the entrance and put his head out.

"What's up, Ratty?" asked the Mole.

"*Snow* is up," replied the Rat briefly, "or rather *down*. It's snowing hard. Well," he continued, "we must make take our chances, I suppose. The worst of it is, I don't know exactly where we are.

And now this snow makes everything look so different."

It did indeed. The Mole came and crouched beside the Rat, and saw the wood that had been so dreadful to him was now quite changed. All the scary holes, hollows, and pools had vanished, and a gleaming white carpet had sprung up everywhere. The Mole would not have known it was the same wood. However, they set out bravely and took the route that seemed most promising. An hour or two later—they had lost all count of time—they sat down on a fallen tree trunk to recover their breath. They were aching with fatigue and bruised with tumbles. They had fallen into several holes and were wet through, and the snow was getting so deep that they could hardly drag their little legs through it. There seemed to be no way out.

"We can't sit here very long," said the Rat.

"The cold is too awful for anything, and the snow is getting so deep. We'll make our way down into that dell and find some sort of shelter, a cave or a hole with a dry floor to it. We'll have a good rest before we try again."

So they struggled down into the dell, where they hunted about for a dry shelter. Suddenly, the Mole tripped and fell forward on his face with a squeal.

"O, my leg!" he cried. "O, my poor shin!" and he sat up on the snow and nursed his leg in both of his front paws. "I must have tripped over a hidden branch or a stump," said the Mole miserably. "O my! O my!"

"It's a very clean cut," said the Rat, examining Mole's leg. "That was never done by a branch or a stump. Looks as if it was made by a sharp edge of something in metal. Funny!"

He pondered awhile, and examined the humps

and slopes that surrounded them. He scratched and shoveled and explored, all four legs working busily, while the Mole waited, impatiently muttering, "O, *come* on, Rat!"

Suddenly, the Rat cried, "Hooray!" and then "Hooray—oo—ray—ray—oo—ray!" and did a silly dance in the snow.

"What *have* you found, Ratty?" asked the Mole, still nursing his leg.

"Come and see!" said the delighted Rat, as he danced on.

The Mole hobbled up to the spot and had a good look.

"Well," he said at last, slowly, "I *see* it right enough. A door scraper! So?"

"But don't you see what it *means*, you—you dull-witted animal?" cried the Rat impatiently.

"Of course, I see what it means," replied the Mole. "Some *very* careless and forgetful person has left his door scraper lying about in the middle of the Wild Wood, *just* where it's *sure* to trip *everybody* up. Very thoughtless of him."

"O dear! O dear!" cried the Rat, in despair. "Here, stop arguing and come and scrape!" And he set to work again and made the snow fly in all directions around him.

The Rat attacked a snowbank beside them, digging with fury; and the Mole scraped busily, too, more to oblige the Rat than for any other reason, for his opinion was that his friend was getting light-headed.

After ten minutes of hard work, Rat struck something that sounded hollow. He worked harder till he could get a paw through and feel, then he called Mole to come and help him. The two animals dug hard till at last the result of their labors stood in full view of the astonished Mole.

In the side of what had seemed to be a snowbank stood a solid-looking little door, painted a dark green. An iron bell-pull hung by the side, and below it, on a small brass plate, neatly engraved in square capital letters, they could read by the aid of moonlight:

MR. BADGER

The Mole fell backward on the snow from sheer surprise and delight. "Rat!" he cried, "you're a wonder! You figured it out, step by step, in that wise head of yours, from that very moment that I fell and cut my shin. If I only had your head, Ratty—"

"But as you haven't," interrupted the Rat rather unkindly, "I suppose you're going to sit on the snow all night and *talk*? Get up at once and hang on to that bell-pull there, and ring hard as you can while I hammer!"

While the Rat attacked the door with a stick, the Mole sprang up at the bell-pull, clutched it, and swung there, both his feet well off the ground. From quite a long way off, they could faintly hear a deep-toned bell respond.

CHAPTER 7

Mr. Badger

They waited patiently for what seemed like a very long time, stamping in the snow to keep their feet warm. At last they heard the sound of slow shuffling foot- steps approaching the door from the inside.

There was a noise as the bolt shot back, and the door opened a few inches, enough to show a long snout and a pair of sleepy, blinking eyes.

"Now, the *very* next time this happens," said a gruff voice, "I shall be exceedingly angry. Who is it *this* time, disturbing people on such a night? Speak up!"

"O, Badger," cried the Rat, "let us in, please. It's me, Rat, and my friend Mole, and we've lost our way in the snow.

"What, Ratty, my dear little man!" exclaimed the Badger in quite a different voice. "Come along in, both of you, at once. Lost in the snow! And in the Wild Wood, too, and at this time of night! But come in with you."

The two animals stumbled over each other in their eagerness to get inside, and heard the door shut behind them with great joy and relief .

The Badger, who wore a long dressing gown and whose slippers were down at the heel, carried a flat candlestick in his paw. He looked kindly down on them, and patted both their heads. "This is not the sort of night for small animals to be out," he said. "I'm afraid you've been up to some of your pranks again, Ratty. But come along. Come into the kitchen. There's a first-rate fire there, and supper and everything."

He shuffled on in front of them, carrying the light, and they followed him down a long, gloomy passage that finally led to a large firelit kitchen. In the middle of the room stood a long table. At one end of it, where an armchair stood pushed back, were the remains of the Badger's supper. The ruddy brick floor smiled up at the smoky ceiling. Plates on the dresser grinned at pots on the shelf, and the merry firelight flickered and played over everything.

The kindly Badger thrust the friends down to toast themselves at the fire and had them remove their coats and boots. Then he fetched them dressing gowns and slippers, and he bathed the

Mole's shin and mended the cut. In the embracing light and warmth, with weary legs propped up in front of them, it seemed to the storm-driven animals that the cold Wild Wood just outside was miles and miles away.

When they were thoroughly toasted, the Badger summoned them to the table. The Badger sat in his armchair at the head of the table, and nodded at intervals as the animals told their story. He did not seem surprised or shocked at anything. The Mole began to feel very friendly toward him.

When supper was finally finished, they gathered around the great wood fire and thought how jolly it was to be sitting up *so* late and *so* full. After they had chatted for some time about things in general, the Badger said heartily, "Now then! Tell us the news from your part of the world. How's old Toad getting along?"

"O, from bad to worse," said the Rat gravely.

"Another smash-up only last week, and a bad one. You see, he's convinced he's a heaven-born driver, and nobody can teach him anything, and all the rest follows."

"How many has he had?" inquired the Badger gloomily.

"Smashes or machines?" asked the Rat. "O, well, after all it's the same thing with Toad. This is the seventh. You know that coach house of his? Well, it's piled up with fragments of motorcars, none of them bigger than your hat!"

"He's been in the hospital three times," put in the Mole; "and as for the fines he's had to pay, it's simply awful to think of."

"Yes, and that's part of the trouble," continued the Rat. "Toad's rich, we all know, but he's not a millionaire. Badger! We're his friends—we should do something!"

The Badger went through a bit of hard thinking. "Now look here!" he said at last, rather severely. "Of course you know I can't do anything *now*?"

The two friends quite understood his point. No animal, according to the rules of animal etiquette, is ever expected to do anything strenuous, or even moderately active, during the off-season of winter. All the animals in winter are sleepy—and some are actually asleep.

"Well, *then*," went on the Badger, "once the year has really turned, we—that is, you and me and our friend the Mole—we'll all take Toad seriously in hand. We'll *make* him be a sensible Toad. We'll . . . you're asleep! Rat!"

"Not me!" said the Rat, waking up with a jerk.

"He's been asleep two or three times since supper," said the Mole, laughing. He himself was feeling quite awake. Being an underground animal, the situation of Badger's house made him feel at home. But the Rat, who slept every night in a bedroom with windows that opened up on a breezy river, was not as comfortable with such a dark underground place.

"Well, it's time we were all in bed," said the Badger, getting up and fetching candlesticks. "Come along, you two, and I'll show you where you'll be sleeping. And take your time tomorrow morning—breakfast at any hour you please!"

He led the two animals to a long room that seemed half bedroom and half loft. The Badger's winter stores took up half the room—piles of apples, turnips, and potatoes, baskets full of nuts, and jars of honey. But the two little white beds on the remainder of the floor looked soft and inviting. The Mole and the Water Rat, shaking off their clothes in some thirty seconds, tumbled into their beds with great joy.

The two tired animals came down to breakfast very late the next morning and found a bright fire burning in the kitchen. Rat cut some bacon, while the Mole dropped some eggs into a saucepan and warmed the coffeepot over the fire. Badger, having already eaten a hearty breakfast, had retired to his study and settled in his armchair with his legs up. He had a red cotton handkerchief over his face, and was being "busy" in his usual way for this time of year.

When the Badger finally entered, yawning and rubbing his eyes, he greeted them in his quiet, simple way. Mole took the opportunity to tell Badger how comfortable and home-like it all felt to him. "Once well underground," he said, "you know exactly where you are. Things go on all the same overhead and you don't bother about them."

The Badger simply beamed at him. "That's exactly what I say," he replied. "There's no security, or peace and tranquillity, except underground. This is my idea of home!"

The Mole agreed heartily, and the Badger got very friendly with him. But the Rat was walking up and down, very restless. The underground atmosphere was getting on his nerves, and he seemed really to be afraid that the river would run away if he wasn't in his own home to look after it. "Come along, Mole," he said anxiously. "We must get off, while it's daylight. Don't want to spend another night in the Wild Wood again."

"You really needn't fret, Ratty," said the Badger calmly. "My passages run farther than you think, though I don't care for everybody to know about them. When you really have to go, you shall leave by one of my shortcuts. Meantime, make yourself comfortable and sit down again."

The Rat was still anxious to get home, so the Badger, taking up his lantern again, led the way along a damp and airless tunnel for a weary distance that seemed like miles. At last daylight began to show itself through tangled growth overhanging the mouth of the passage, and the

Badger, bidding them a hasty good-bye, pushed them through the opening and retreated.

They found themselves standing on the very edge of the Wild Wood. Rocks and brambles and tree roots lay behind them in tangled heaps. In front of them was a great space of quiet fields, hemmed by lines of hedges, black on the snow. And far ahead was a glint of the familiar old river. Pausing there a moment and looking back, they saw the whole mass of the Wild Wood, dense, menacing, grimly set in vast white surroundings. They turned and headed swiftly for home, for firelight and the familiar things it played on, for the river that they knew and trusted in all its moods.

CHAPTER 8

Dolce Domum

༄

Rat and Mole plodded along steadily, each thinking his own thoughts. The Rat was walking a little way ahead, as his habit was, shoulders slumped, his eyes fixed on the road ahead of him. So he did not notice poor Mole when he stopped suddenly, as if in shock.

We others, who have long lost the most subtle of our physical senses, have only the word *smell* to include the whole range of thrills that murmur in the nose of the animal night and day. It was one of those mysterious calls that suddenly reached Mole in the darkness, making him tingle through and through. He stopped dead in his tracks, his nose searching. A moment later he had caught it again. This time, he knew what it was.

Home! It must be quite close, his old home that he had hurriedly left that day when he first found the river! Now, with a rush of old memories, how clearly it stood up before him in the darkness! Shabby indeed, and small, and yet it was the home he had made for himself, the home he had been so happy to get back to after his day's work. And the home had been happy with him, too, and was missing him and wanted him back.

"Ratty!" he called, full of joyful excitement, "hold on! Come back! I want you, quick! It's my home, my old home! O, slow down, Ratty! Please, please, come back!"

The Rat was by this time very far ahead, too far to hear clearly what the Mole was calling, too far to catch the sharp note of painful appeal

in his voice. He, too, could smell something—
something suspiciously like approaching snow.

"Mole, we mustn't stop now, really!" he called
back. "We'll come for it tomorrow, whatever it is
you've found. But it's late, and the snow's coming
again. I'm not sure of the way! And I want your
nose, Mole, so come on quick, there's a good fellow!" And the Rat pressed forward on his way
without waiting for an answer.

Poor Mole stood alone in the road, his heart
torn and a big sob gathering low down inside him.
But his loyalty to his friend stood firm. Never for
a moment did he dream of abandoning him.
Though he wanted to be home very badly, Mole
set his face down the road and followed in the
track of the Rat.

With some effort he caught up to the unsus-
pecting Rat, who began chattering cheerfully
about what they would do when they got back.
At last, when they had gone some considerable

way farther, he stopped and said kindly, "Look here, Mole, old chap, you seem dead tired. No talk left in you, and your feet dragging like lead. We'll sit down here for a minute to rest. The snow has held off so far, and the best part of our journey is over."

Mole at last gave up the struggle and cried freely and helplessly and openly, now that he knew it was all over and he had lost what he could hardly be said to have found.

The Rat said, very quietly and sympathetically, "What is it, old fellow? Whatever can be the matter?"

Poor Mole found it difficult to get any words out. "I know, it's a—shabby, dingy little place," he sobbed brokenly, "not like—your cozy quarters—or Toad's beautiful hall—or Badger's great house—but it was my own little home—and I went away and forgot all about it—and I smelled it suddenly—on the road, when I called and you wouldn't listen. I thought my heart would break. We might have just gone and had one look at it, Ratty—one look. O dear! O dear!"

The Rat stared straight in front of him, patting Mole gently on the shoulder. "I see it all now! What a *pig* I have been! Just a pig—a plain pig!"

He waited till Mole's sobs became gradually less stormy. Then Rat rose from his seat. "Well," he said, "we'd really better be getting on, old chap!" Rat turned around and set off up the road again, back over the way they had come.

"Wherever are (hic) you going (hic) to, Ratty?"

"We're going to take you home, old fellow," replied the Rat pleasantly, "so you had better come along. We'll need your nose."

Still snuffling, Mole allowed himself to be dragged back along the road while his uplifted nose, quivering slightly, felt the air. Then a short, quick run forward—a fault—a check—a try back, and then a slow, steady confident advance.

Suddenly, without giving much warning, he dived down a tunnel in the ground. But the Rat was on the alert, and promptly followed him.

The passage was close and airless, and the earthy smell was strong, and it seemed like a long time to Rat before it ended and he could stand erect and stretch himself. The Mole struck a match, and by its light the Rat saw that they were standing in an open space, neatly swept and sanded underfoot, directly facing Mole's little door, with MOLE END painted over the bell-pull at the side.

Mole pulled a lantern off a nail on the wall. He hurried Rat through the door, lit a lamp in the hall, and took one glance around his old home. He saw the dust lying thick on everything, saw the cheerless, deserted look of the long-neglected house, and collapsed on a hall chair, his nose in his paws. "O Ratty!" he cried dismally, "why did I

ever do it? Why did I bring you to this poor, cold little place, on a night like this, when you might have been at River Bank, toasting your toes before a blazing fire?"

The Rat ignored this. He was running here and there, lighting lamps and candles and sticking them up everywhere. "We'll make a jolly night of it. Was this your own idea, those sleeping bunks in the wall? Splendid! The first thing we want is a good fire. I'll fetch the wood and the coals, and you get the duster, Mole, and try to smarten things up a bit. Hurry up, old chap!"

The Mole roused himself and dusted and polished with energy and heartiness, while the Rat soon had a cheerful blaze roaring up the chimney. He told Mole to come and warm himself when suddenly sounds were heard from outside—like the scuffling of small feet in the gravel and a confused murmur of tiny voices: "Now, all in a line—hold the lantern up a bit, Tommy—

clear your throats—no coughing after I say *one, two, three*—Where's young Bill?"

"What's up?" inquired the Rat.

"It must be the field mice," replied the Mole. "They go around carol singing regularly at this time of year. It will be like old times to hear them again."

"Let's have a look at them!" cried the Rat, jumping up and running to the door.

Some eight or ten little field mice stood in a semicircle, red scarves around their throats, their forepaws thrust deep into their pockets, their feet jigging for warmth. With bright beady eyes, they glanced shyly at each other, sniggering and sniffing. One of the elder ones who carried a lantern said, "Now then, one, two, three!" and their shrill little voices rose, singing out one of the old-time carols.

Finally, the voices ceased. The singers were bashful but smiling, exchanging sidelong glances.

"Very well sung, boys!" cried the Rat heartily. "And now come along in, all of you. Warm yourselves by the fire, and have something hot!"

"Yes, come along, field mice," cried the Mole eagerly. "This is quite like old times! Shut the door after you. Pull up to the fire. Now, you just wait a minute, while we—O Ratty!" he cried in despair. "Whatever are we doing? We've nothing to give them!"

"You leave all that to me," said the masterful Rat. "Here, you with the lantern! Come over this way. Now, tell me, are there any shops open at this hour of night?"

"Why certainly, sir," replied the field mouse respectfully. "At this time of the year our shops stay open to all sorts of hours."

"Then look here!" said the Rat. "You go off at once, you and your lantern, and you get me—"

Here much muttered conversation followed. Finally, there was a clink of coins passing from paw to paw, the field mouse was given a basket for his purchases, and off he hurried with his lantern.

The rest of the field mice perched in a row on a bench, their small legs swinging, and gave themselves up to the enjoyment of the fire.

Finally, the latch clicked, the door opened, and the field mouse reappeared, staggering under the weight of his basket. Everybody was told to do something or to fetch something. In a very few minutes, supper was ready. As they ate, they talked of old times, and the field mice gave Mole and Rat the local gossip update and answered as well as they could the hundred questions they had to ask them.

They clattered off at last, very grateful and showering wishes of the season, with their jacket pockets stuffed with treats for the small brothers and sisters at home. When the door had closed on the last of them, Mole and Rat added wood to the fire, drew their chairs in, and discussed the events of the long day. At last the Rat, with a great yawn, said, "Mole, old chap, I'm ready to drop. Is that your bunk over on that side? Very well then, I'll take this."

He clambered into his bunk, rolled himself well up in the blanket, and was soon asleep. The weary Mole was also glad to turn in and soon had his head on the pillow, in great joy and contentment. Before he closed his eyes, he let them wander around his old room, mellow in the glow of firelight that played or rested on familiar and friendly things that had long been a part of him. He saw clearly how much it all meant to him. He did not want to abandon his new life, to turn his back on the sun and air and all they offered him. But it was good to think he had returned to this place that was all his own, these things that were so glad to see him again and could always be counted upon for the same simple welcome.

CHAPTER 9

Mr. Toad

‿౸

It was a bright morning in the early part of the summer. A hot sun seemed to be pulling everything green and bushy up out of the earth. The Mole and the Water Rat had been up since dawn, busy on matters connected with the opening of boating season: painting, mending paddles, repairing cushions, and so on. They were finishing breakfast in their little parlor when a heavy knock sounded at the door.

The Mole went to answer it, and the Rat heard

THE WIND IN THE WILLOWS

him utter a cry of surprise. The Badger strode heavily into the room. The Rat let his spoon fall on the tablecloth, and sat openmouthed.

"The hour has come!" said the Badger at last.

"What hour?" asked the Rat uneasily, glancing at the clock on the mantel.

"*Whose* hour, you should rather say," replied the Badger. "Why, the hour of Toad!"

"Toad's hour, of course!" cried the Mole delightedly. "We planned last winter to teach him to be a sensible Toad!"

"Right you are!" cried the Rat, jumping up. "We'll rescue the poor, unhappy animal! We'll convert him! He'll be the most converted Toad that ever was before we're done with him!"

They reached the carriage drive of Toad Hall to find a shiny new motorcar, of great size and painted bright red, sitting in front of the house. As they neared the house, the door was flung open and Mr. Toad, in goggles, cap, and enormous overcoat, came swaggering down the steps, drawing on his gloves.

"Hullo! Come on, you fellows!" he cried cheerfully as he saw them. "You're just in time to come with me for a jolly—uhm—er—jolly—"

His smile fell away as he noticed the serious look on the faces of his silent friends. The Badger strode up the steps. "Take him inside," he said sternly to his companions. Then Toad was hustled through the door, struggling and protesting.

"Now then!" Badger said to the Toad when the four of them together stood in the hall. "First of all, take those ridiculous things off!"

"I won't!" replied Toad, with great spirit. "What is the meaning of this outrage?"

"Take them off him then," ordered the Badger.

Then the Rat and the Mole got Toad's motor clothes off bit by bit, and they stood him on his legs again. Now that he was merely Toad, and no longer the Terror of the Highway, he giggled feebly, seeming to understand the situation.

"You knew it must come to this, sooner or later, Toad," the Badger explained severely. "You've spent all the money your father left you, and you're getting us animals a bad name by your smashes and fights with the police. Now you will come with me and hear some hard facts about yourself."

He took Toad firmly by the arm, led him into another room, and closed the door behind him. After some three-quarters of an hour, the door opened, and the Badger reappeared, leading by the paw a very dejected Toad. His legs wobbled and his cheeks were furrowed by tears.

"Sit down there, Toad," said the Badger kindly, pointing to a chair. "My friends," he went on, "I am pleased to inform you that Toad has, at last, seen the error of his ways. He had under- taken to give up motorcars entirely and forever."

"That is very good news," said the Mole gravely.

"There's only one more thing more to be done," continued the Badger. "Toad, I want you to repeat, before your friends, what you fully admitted to me just now. First, you are sorry for what you have done, and you see the folly of it all."

There was a long, long pause. Toad looked this way and that while the other animals waited in silence.

"No!" he said a little sullenly. "I'm *not* sorry. And it wasn't folly at all! It was simply glorious!"

"What?" cried the Badger. "Didn't you tell me just now, in there——?"

"O yes, in *there*," said Toad impatiently. "I'd have said anything in *there*. But I've been searching my mind since, and I find that I'm not a bit sorry."

"Then you don't promise," said the Badger, "never to touch a motorcar again?"

"Certainly not! On the contrary, I promise that the very first motorcar I see—poop-poop!—off I go in it!"

"Very well, then," said the Badger firmly, rising to his feet. "I feared it would come to this all along. You've often asked us three to come and stay with you, Toad, in this handsome house of yours. Well, now we're going to. Take him upstairs, you two, and lock him up in his bedroom."

"It's for your own good, Toady, you know," said the Rat kindly, as Toad, kicking and struggling, was hauled up the stairs by his two friends.

"We'll take great care of everything for you till you're well, Toad," said the Mole.

"No more of those regrettable incidents with the police, Toad," said the Rat as they thrust him into his bedroom.

They came back downstairs, Toad shouting abuse at them through the keyhole, and the three friends then met to talk about the situation.

"It's going to be hard," said the Badger, sighing. "I've never seen Toad so determined. However, we shall see it out, till the poison has worked itself out of his system."

Each animal took it in turns to sleep in Toad's room at night, and they divided the day up among them. At first Toad was very difficult with his careful guardians. He would arrange bedroom chairs to look like a motorcar and stare straight ahead, making terrible noises. As time passed, however, this happened less and less. But his spirits did not seem to revive, and he grew depressed.

CHAPTER 10

Escape and Ruin

ᥳᢀ

One fine morning, Rat went upstairs to relieve Badger. "Toad's still in bed," he told the Rat, outside the door. "Now, you look out! When Toad's quiet and cooperative, there's sure to be something up. I know him."

"How are you today, old chap?" inquired the Rat cheerfully, as he approached Toad's bedside.

After a few minutes, a feeble voice replied, "Thank you so much, dear Ratty! But first, how are you yourself and the excellent Mole?"

"O, *we're* all right," replied the Rat. "Mole is

going out for a run around with Badger. So you and I will spend a pleasant morning together. Don't lie there moping on a fine morning like this."

"Dear, kind, Rat," murmured Toad, "how little you understand me. I hate being a burden to my friends, but I do not expect to be one much longer."

"Well, I hope not, too," said the Rat heartily. "You've been a real bother. But I'd take any trouble on earth for you, if only you'd be a more sensible animal."

"If this is true," murmured Toad, more feebly than ever, "then I must beg you to step around to the village—even if it may be too late—and fetch the doctor."

"Why, what do you want the doctor for?" inquired the Rat, coming closer and examining him. Toad's voice was weaker, and his manner was very different.

"Surely, you have noticed lately—" murmured Toad. "We must act quickly. Tomorrow, indeed, you may be saying to yourself, 'O, if only I had noticed sooner! If only I had done something!'"

"Look here, old friend," said the Rat, beginning to get rather alarmed, "of course I'll fetch a doctor. But you can hardly be bad enough for that yet. Let's talk about something else."

"I fear, dear Rat," said Toad, with a sad smile, "that 'talk' can do little in a case like this—or doctors, either, for that matter. And by the way— while you are about it—would you mind asking the lawyer to stop by?"

"A lawyer! O, he must be really bad!" the scared Rat said to himself. He hurried from the room, not forgetting, however, to lock the door behind him.

The Toad hopped lightly out of bed as soon as he heard the key turned in the lock, and watched

Rat eagerly from the window till he disappeared
down the drive. Then he dressed as quickly as possible, in the smartest suit he could lay hands on,
and filled his pockets with cash. Next, knot-
ting the sheets together and tying one end
around the frame of the window, he
scrambled out, and slid lightly to the
ground. Taking the opposite
direction to the Rat,
Toad marched off light-
heartedly, whistling a
merry tune.

Later, it was a gloomy
lunch for Rat when he had
to face the Badger and the
Mole. Meanwhile, Toad
was walking briskly
along the road, some
miles from home.
Feeling safe, and the

sun smiling brightly on him, he almost danced along the road in satisfaction.

"Smart piece of work!" he remarked to himself, chuckling. "Poor old Ratty! Won't he get in trouble when Badger gets back! A worthy fellow, Ratty, with many good qualities, but very little intelligence."

Filled full of mean thoughts such as these, he walked along, his head in the air, till he reached a little inn on the edge of town. The sign of THE RED LION reminded him that he was very hungry after his long walk. He marched into the inn, ordered the best lunch that could be provided, and sat down to eat it.

He was about halfway through his meal when a familiar sound made him start trembling all over. The "poop-poop!" sound drew nearer and nearer. The car could be heard to turn into the yard and come to the stoop, and Toad had to hold on to the leg of the table to keep from jumping with excitement. Soon the party entered the room, hungry and talkative. Toad could stand it no longer. He slipped out of the room quietly and, as soon as he got outside, walked around quietly to the yard. "There cannot be any harm," he said to himself, "in only just *looking* at it."

The car stood in the middle of the yard. Toad walked slowly around it. The next moment, hardly knowing how it came about, he found he had hold of the door handle and was turning it. As if in a dream he found himself seated in the driver's seat. As if in a dream, he swung the car around the yard. As if in a dream, all sense of right and wrong seemed suspended. As the car devoured the street and leaped forth on the high road through the open country, all he knew was that he was Toad once more, Toad the Terror!

CHAPTER 11

Toad Faces the Judge

⸺

Toad didn't remember the accident that followed; nor did he remember the police who arrested him. The rush of the open road possessed him completely, fading only when Toad found himself in the courtroom and heard the judge call his name.

"To my mind," observed the judge cheerfully, "this hardened ruffian has been found guilty, first, of stealing a motorcar; second, of driving to the public danger; and third, of gross impertinence to the police. Prisoner! It's going to be ten years for you this time. And mind, if you appear before us again, we shall have to deal with you very seriously!"

The brutal minions of the law fell upon the hapless Toad, loaded him with chains, and dragged him from the courthouse, and down the street, till they reached the door of the grimmest dungeon that lay in the heart of the jail. There an ancient jailer sat fingering a bunch of mighty keys.

"Rouse," said the sergeant of police, "take over from us this vile Toad, a criminal of deepest guilt. Watch and guard him with all your skill!"

The jailer nodded grimly, laying his withered hand on the shoulder of the miserable Toad. The rusty key creaked in the lock, the great door closed behind them, and Toad was a helpless prisoner.

CHAPTER 12

The Piper at the Gates of Dawn

໒ာ

Mole lay stretched on the bank, waiting for his friend Rat to return. It was past ten o'clock at night, but it was still too hot to think of staying inside. The Rat's light footsteps were soon heard approaching.

"You stayed at Otter's for supper, of course," said the Mole presently.

"Simply had to," said the Rat. "Mole, I'm afraid they're in trouble. Little Portly is missing again; and you know what a lot Otter thinks of him, though he never says much about it."

"What, that child?" said the Mole lightly. "He's always straying off and getting lost, and turning up again."

"Yes, but this time it's more serious," said the Rat gravely. "He's been missing for some time now, and the otters have hunted everywhere without finding the slightest trace. Otter was going to spend the night watching by the shallow part of the river. You know the place where the old fort used to be, before they built the bridge?"

"I know it well," said the Mole.

"Well, it seems that it was there he gave Portly his first swimming lesson," continued the Rat. "And it was there he used to teach him fishing, and there young Portly caught his first fish, which made him very proud. The child loves the spot, and so Otter is there now, waiting—on the chance, you know, just the chance. . . ."

They were silent for a time, both thinking of the same thing—the lonely animal, crouched by the riverbank, watching and waiting the long night through.

"Rat," said the Mole, "I simply can't turn in and go to sleep and *do* nothing. We'll get the boat out and paddle upstream. The moon will be up in an hour or so, and then we will search as well as we can."

"Just what I was thinking myself," said the Rat.

They got the boat out, and Rat took the oars, paddling with caution. At last, the moon lifted with slow majesty till it swung clear of the horizon. Fastening their boat to a willow, the friends landed in this silent, silver kingdom and patiently explored the ditches and old dry riverbeds. Embarking again, they worked their way up the stream in this manner, till the moon sank earthward and left them in the early morning.

The horizon became clearer, fields and trees came more into sight, and the mystery began to drop away from them. A bird piped up suddenly, but it was a song like nothing Rat had ever heard. He listened closely. Mole, who was just keeping the boat moving with gentle strokes, didn't hear it. He looked at Rat with curiosity.

"It's gone!" sighed the Rat, sinking back in his seat again. He was truly enchanted by the magical sound. "I almost wish I had never heard it. Nothing seems worthwhile but just to hear that sound once more and go on listening to it forever. There it is again!" he cried. "O, Mole! The beauty of it. Such music I never dreamed of. Row on, Mole, row!"

Mole still hadn't heard the sound, but he rowed steadily and soon they came to a point where the creeping tide of light gained and gained, and now they could see the color of the flowers at the water's edge.

"Clearer and nearer still," cried the Rat joyously. "Now you must surely hear it!"

Breathless, the Mole stopped rowing as the sound of glad piping broke on him like a wave. It wasn't a birdsong at all. Still, it was a song as beautiful as any bird, as beautiful as any sound Rat and Mole had ever heard.

Slowly, but with no doubt or hesitation whatever, they tied up their boat at the flowery edge of the island. In silence, they landed and pushed through the undergrowth that led up to the level ground, till they stood on a little lawn of a marvelous green, set around with orchard trees— crab apple and wild cherry.

Suddenly, the Mole felt such a great wonder fall up on him that he bowed his head, and rooted his feet to the ground. They both felt they were in the presence of a great power. Mole turned to look for his friend, and saw him at his side, trembling violently. There was utter silence in the bird-filled branches.

Mole could not help but raise his eyes, even

though he was shaking with fear. He found himself looking into the eyes of a magnificent new creature. Mole saw the backward sweep of a curved horn, gleaming in the growing daylight. He saw kindly eyes that were looking down on them humorously, while a bearded mouth broke into a half smile. And he saw a long hand holding a gleaming set of pipes. Finally, he saw the splendid curves of shaggy limbs and, nestling between the creature's hooves, the round form of the missing baby Otter sleeping safely and soundly in peace.

Sudden and magnificent, the sun's golden disk showed itself over the horizon. The first rays that shot across the level water took the animals full in the eyes and dazzled them. When they were able to look once more, the creature had vanished.

Portly the Otter woke up with a joyous squeak, and wriggled with pleasure at the sight of his father's friends, who had played with him so often in past days. The Rat looked long and doubtfully at hoof marks deep in the ground.

"Some great animal has been here," he murmured thoughtfully. For a long while, neither he nor Mole said anything.

"Come along, Rat!" called the Mole finally. "Think of poor Otter, waiting by the riverbank."

As they drew near the familiar riverbank, they lifted Portly out and set him on his legs on the path toward his father, gave him a farewell pat on the back, and shoved out into midstream. They watched the little animal as he waddled along the path contentedly. Looking up the river, they could see the Otter start up, tense and rigid, and could hear his joyous bark as he bounded up on to the path. As they rowed home up the river, both animals thought of the magnificent creature they had seen, the power of its strange music, and the way it had led them to Portly.

Rat wanted to say something to Mole, and Mole wanted to say something to Rat, but neither could think of words for what they had seen. So they paddled along in silence, comforted by the calmness and peacefulness of the early morning.

CHAPTER 13

Toad's Adventures

つ

Meanwhile, Toad found himself in a dank dungeon. He flung himself at full length on the floor and abandoned himself to dark despair. "This is the end of everything," he said. "At least it is the end of Toad, which is the same thing." With cries such as these, he passed his days and nights, refusing his meals.

Now, the jailer had a daughter, who was particularly fond of animals. One day, she knocked at the door on Toad's cell.

"Cheer up, Toad," she said on entering, "and

sit up and dry your eyes and be a sensible animal. And do try to eat a bit of dinner. See, I've brought you some of mine, hot from the oven."

The smell of cabbage reached the nose of Toad. But he refused to be comforted. The wise girl left for the time, but a good deal of the cabbage smell remained.

When the girl returned, some hours later, she carried a tray with a cup of hot tea steaming on it, and a plate piled up with buttered toast, the butter running off in great drops, like honey from the honeycomb. Toad sat up, dried his eyes, and sipped his tea. He munched his toast and soon began talking about himself.

"Tell me about Toad Hall," the girl said. "But first wait till I fetch some more tea and toast."

She soon returned with a fresh tray. Toad, his spirits quite restored, told her all about his house, and the fun he had when the other animals were gathered around. She wanted to know about his animal friends, and how they lived, and what they did. Of course, she did not say she was fond of animals as *pets*, because she had the sense to see that Toad would be extremely offended.

They had many interesting talks together, after that, as the dreary days went on. The jailer's daughter grew very sorry for Toad and thought it was a great shame that a poor little animal should be locked up in prison for what seemed like a trivial offense.

"Toad," she said one morning, "I have an aunt who does the washing for all of the prisoners here. She takes the washing out on Monday morning and brings it in on Friday morning. Today is Thursday. Now, I believe I could dress you up in her dress and bonnet and you could escape from the jail. You're alike in many respects—particularly about the figure."

"We're *not*," said the Toad in a huff. "I have a very elegant figure—for what I am."

"So has my aunt," replied the girl, "for what *she* is. But have it your own way. You horrid, proud, ungrateful animal, when I'm trying to help you."

"Yes, yes," said the Toad. "But look here! You couldn't possibly have Mr. Toad of Toad Hall going about dressed as a washerwoman!"

"Then you can stay here as Toad!" replied the girl with much spirit.

"You are a good, kind, clever girl," Toad said, "and I am indeed a proud and stupid Toad. Introduce me to your worthy aunt, if you will be so kind."

The next evening, the girl ushered her aunt into Toad's cell. The old lady had been prepared for the meeting, and the sight of the gold coins that Toad had placed on the table left little further to discuss. In return for his cash, Toad received a cotton print gown, an apron, a shawl, and a black bonnet.

Shaking with laughter, the girl fit him into the gown, arranged the shawl, and tied the strings of the bonnet under his chin.

"You look just like her," she giggled. "Only, I'm sure you never looked so respectable in all your life before. Now, good-bye, Toad, and good luck."

With a quaking heart, Toad set forth on what seemed to be a most hazardous trip, but he was soon surprised at how easy everything was. The costume seemed a key for every locked door and grim gateway. At last he heard the gate in the great outer door click behind him, felt the fresh air of the outer world upon his brow, and knew that he was free!

He walked quickly toward the lights of the town. As he ambled along, his attention was caught by some red and green lights a little way off, to one side of town. He heard the sound of train engines puffing and snorting.

"Aha!" he thought, "this is a piece of luck! A railway station is the thing I want most in the whole world at this moment."

He made his way to the station and found that a train, bound more or less in the direction of his home, was due to leave in half an hour. "More luck!" said Toad, his spirits rising rapidly, and went off to buy his ticket.

He gave the name of that station he knew to be nearest to Toad Hall and put his fingers where his waistcoat pocket should have been, in search of the money for the ticket. But then he realized that he had not only no money, but no pocket to hold it, and no waistcoat to hold the pocket!

To his horror, he remembered that he had left both his coat and waistcoat behind him in his cell, and with them his money, keys, and watch—all that makes life worth living.

Full of despair, he wandered blindly down the platform where the train was standing, and tears trickled down each side of his nose. Very soon, his escape would be discovered, and he would be caught and dragged back to prison. What was to be done?

"Hullo, mother!" said the engine driver. "What's the trouble? You don't look particularly cheerful."

"O, sir!" said Toad, crying. "I am a poor, unhappy washerwoman, and I've lost all my money, and can't pay for a ticket, and I *must* get home tonight somehow. O dear, O dear!"

"That's a bad business, indeed," said the engine driver. "Lost your money—and can't get home—and got some kids, too, waiting for you, I daresay?"

"Any amount of 'em," sobbed Toad. "And they'll be hungry—and playing with matches— and upsetting lamps, the little ones! O dear, O dear!"

"Well, I'll tell you what I'll do," said the good

engine driver. "You're a washerwoman. Very well. And I'm an engine driver, as you may well see, and there's no denying it's terribly dirty work. If you'll wash a few shirts for me when you get home, and send 'em along, I'll give you a ride on my engine."

The Toad's misery turned into joy as he eagerly scrambled up into the cab of the engine. Of course, he had never washed a shirt in his life, but he thought, "When I get safely home to Toad Hall, I will send the engine driver enough to pay for a lot of washing, and that will be the same thing or better."

The guard waved his welcome flag, the engine driver whistled in cheerful response, and the train moved out of the station. As the speed increased, and Toad could see on either side of him real fields, and trees, and hedges, and cows, and horses, all flying past him, he thought how every minute was bringing him nearer to Toad Hall. He began to skip up and down, and shout and sing, to the great astonishment of the engine driver, who had come across washerwomen before, but never one at all like this.

They had covered many a mile when Toad noticed that the engine driver, with a puzzled expression on his face, was leaning over the side of the engine and listening hard. "It's very strange. We're the last train running in this direction tonight, yet I hear another following us!"

Toad stopped his silly antics at once. He became serious and depressed, and a dull pain in the lower part of his spine made him want to sit down and try desperately not to think of all the possibilities.

Presently, the engine driver called out, "I can see it clearly now! It is an engine, on our rails. They are gaining on us fast! And the engine is crowded with policemen in their helmets waving clubs, detectives waving revolvers and walking sticks, all waving, and all shouting the same thing—'Stop, stop, stop!'"

The Toad fell on his knees among the coals, raised his clasped paws, and cried, "Save me, only save me, dear kind Mr. Engine Driver. I am not the simple washerwoman I seem to be! I am a Toad—the well-known and popular Mr. Toad. I have just escaped, by my great daring and cleverness, from a loathsome dungeon, and if those fellows on that engine recapture me, it will be chains and bread and water and straw and misery once more for poor, innocent Toad!"

The engine driver looked down at him sternly, and said, "Now tell the truth. What were you in prison for?"

"It was nothing much," said poor Toad. "I only borrowed a motorcar while the owners were at lunch. I didn't mean to steal it, really, but people take such harsh views of my high-spirited actions."

The engine driver looked very severe. "I fear that you have been a wicked Toad. But the sight of an animal in tears makes me feel softhearted. So cheer up, Toad! We may beat them yet!"

They piled on more coal, shoveling furiously. The furnace roared, the sparks flew, but still their pursuers slowly gained. The engine driver, with a sigh, wiped his brow. "There's one thing left, and it's your only chance. A short way ahead of us is a long tunnel, and on the other side the line rail passes through the thick wood. Now, when we are through, I will put on the brakes as hard as I can, and you must jump and hide in the wood before they get through the tunnel and see you. Then I will go full speed again, and they can chase *me* if they like."

The train shot into the tunnel and out the other end into the fresh air and the peaceful moonlight. The driver shut off steam and put on brakes. As the train slowed down, Toad heard the driver call out, "Now jump!"

Toad jumped, rolled down a short hill, picked himself up unhurt, scrambled into the wood, and hid. Peeping out, he saw his train get up speed again and disappear at a great pace. Then out of the tunnel burst the train of police, roaring and whistling, the crew shouting, "Stop! Stop!"

He did not dare leave the shelter of the trees, so he fled into the wood, with the idea of leaving the railway as far as possible behind. After being in jail, he found the wood strange and unfriendly. At last, cold, hungry, and tired out, he found shelter in a hollow tree, where he made himself as comfortable a bed as he could and slept soundly till the morning.

CHAPTER 14

Wayfarers All

cᴐ

The Water Rat was restless, and he did not know exactly why. Leaving the waterside, he wandered, crossed a field or two, already looking dusty and dry, and thrust into the great field of wheat. Here he had many small friends. Today, however, the field mice and harvest mice seemed busy. Many were digging and tunneling. Others examined plans and drawings of small homes. Some were already elbow-deep in packing their belongings.

"Here's old Ratty!" they cried as soon as they saw him.

"What sort of games are you up to?" said the Water Rat. "You know it isn't time to be thinking of winter plans yet, by a long way!"

"O yes, we know that," explained a field mouse, rather bashfully. "But we really *must* get all the furniture and baggage and stores moved out of this before those horrid machines begin clicking around the fields."

"O, bother," said the Rat. "It's a splendid day. Come for a row, or a stroll along the hedges."

"Well, I *think* not, thank you," replied the field mouse hurriedly. "In an hour or two we might be able to join you."

"You won't be free until Christmas with all this work! I can see that," retorted the Rat grumpily as he picked his way out of the field.

He returned somewhat sadly to his river again—his faithful, steady old river, which never packed up or went into winter hiding. By the bank, he spied a swallow sitting. Soon it was joined by another, and then a third. The birds, fidgeting restlessly, talked together seriously and low.

"You're not getting ready for winter, too?" said the Rat, strolling up to them. "What's the hurry? I call it simply ridiculous."

"O, we're not leaving yet," replied the first swallow. "We're only making plans—what route we're taking this year, and where we'll stop, and so on. That's half the fun!"

"Fun?" said the Rat. "Now that's just what I don't understand."

"No, you don't understand, naturally," said the second swallow. "We feel it stirring within us as one by one the scents and sounds and names of long-forgotten places come gradually back and beckon to us."

"Couldn't you stop for just this year?" suggested the Water Rat, worried about a lonely winter ahead. "You have no idea what good times we have here, while you're far away."

"I tried stopping one year," said the third swallow. "For a few weeks it was all well enough, but afterward, O, the weary length of the nights! The shivering, sunless days! No, it was no good. My courage broke down and one cold, stormy night I took wing and moved southward."

"Why do you ever come back at all?" Rat demanded of the swallows jealously. "What do you find to attract you in this drab little country?"

"Do you really think," said the first swallow, "that the north doesn't call us, too, in its due season? In time, we shall be homesick once more for quiet water lilies swaying on the surface of the stream."

They fell a-twittering among themselves once more. Restlessly, the Rat wandered off. He climbed the slope that rose gently from the bank of the river. On this side, he looked into the distance and dreamed of traveling himself. What seas lay beyond? What sunbathed coasts and quiet harbors?

Footsteps fell on his ear, and a tired figure came into view. He saw that it was another Rat, and a very dusty one. The wayfarer saluted with a friendly wave and sat down by his side. He was lean and somewhat bowed at the shoulders. His paws were thin and long, his eyes much wrinkled at the corners.

When he had rested awhile the stranger sighed, sniffed the air, and looked about him.

"That was clover, the warm whiff on the breeze," he remarked. "And those are cows we hear eating the grass behind us and blowing softly between mouthfuls. Everything seems asleep, and yet going on all the time. It is a good life that you lead, friend."

"Yes, it's *the* life, the only life to live," responded the Water Rat dreamily.

"I did not say that exactly," replied the stranger cautiously. "I've just tried it—six months of it. Here I am, leaving it, following the call back to the old life, *the* life, which will not let me go."

"You are not one of *us*," said the Water Rat, "nor a farmer. You are not even from this country."

"Right," replied the stranger. "I'm a seafaring rat, I am. The city of my birth is no more my home than any port between there and the London River. I know them all and they know me. Set me down on any shore and I am home again."

"I suppose you go on great voyages," said the Water Rat with growing interest. "Months and months out of sight of land, and your mind communing with the mighty ocean, and all that sort of thing."

"By no means," said the Sea Rat. "It's the jolly times on shore that appeal to me. O those southern seaports! The smell of them, the lights at night, the glamour!"

"Well, perhaps you have chosen the better way," said the Water Rat, but rather doubtfully. "Tell me something of your travels."

The Sea Rat told the story of his latest voyage, conducting the Water Rat from port to port with his tale, landing him at Lisbon and Bordeaux, introducing him to the pleasant harbors of Cornwall and Devon, and up the channel to London. Quivering with excitement, the Water Rat was captivated. The seafarer's eyes lit with a brightness as he leaned toward Rat and kept him fascinated, powerless.

The stranger's words held a powerful spell. As Rat listened, he became hypnotized by the deep voice and the mysterious adventures it described. The quiet world he knew and loved faded far away and ceased to be. And as the wonderful talk flowed on, Rat fell more and more under the power of this spell. But soon the adventurer rose to his feet, still speaking, still holding the Water Rat fast with his sea-gray eyes.

"And now," he said softly, "I take to the road again, till at last I reach the little gray sea town I know so well. And you, you will come, too, young brother, for the days pass, and never return, and the south still waits for you. Take the adventure, heed the call, before the moment passes!"

The voice died away and ceased. The Water Rat rose without thinking. He returned home, gathered together a few small items, and put them carefully in a bag, moving about the room like a sleepwalker. He swung the bag over his shoulder and stepped across the threshold just as Mole appeared at the door.

"Why, where are you off to, Ratty?" asked the Mole in great surprise, grabbing him by the arm.

"Going south with the rest of them," murmured the Rat in a dreamy voice, never looking at him. "Seaward first and then on a ship, and to the shores that are calling me."

He pressed forward, but the Mole placed himself in front of him. Looking into his eyes, he saw that they were glazed and set. It was like seeing the eyes of some other animal! Grappling with him strongly, Mole dragged Rat inside, threw him down, and held him.

The Rat struggled desperately for a few moments, and then his strength seemed to leave him, and he lay still and exhausted, with closed eyes, trembling. The Mole placed him in a chair, where he sat collapsed, his whole body shivering. Gradually, the Rat sank into a troubled doze.

The Mole left him for a time and busied himself with household matters. It was getting dark when he returned to the parlor and found the Rat where he had left him, wide awake but silent and dejected. Mole took one glance at Rat's eyes and was happy to find them clear and dark and brown as before.

Poor Ratty did his best to explain things, but how could he put into cold words what had mostly been suggestion? Even to himself now, the spell was broken and the glamour was gone, he found it difficult to account for what had seemed, some hours ago, the only thing.

To the Mole, this much was plain: The fit or attack had passed away. Casually, then, he turned his talk to the harvest that was being gathered in, and the large moon rising over bare acres. He talked of reddening apples, of the browning nuts, of jams and preserves—all the things Rat loved best. Mole soon brought Rat out of the spell and back to the joys of their snug home life.

The Rat began to sit up and to join in. His dull eyes brightened, and he lost some of his listless air. It was a joy to the Mole to know that the cure had at least begun.

CHAPTER 15

The Further Adventures of Toad

တာ

Toad was awakened at an early hour, partly by the bright sunlight streaming in on him and partly by the coldness of his toes, which made him dream he was at home in bed in his own handsome room.

Sitting up, he rubbed his eyes first and his complaining toes next. He wondered for a moment where he was, looking around for a familiar stone wall and a little barred window. Then, with a leap of the heart, he remembered everything.

Free! The word and the thought alone were worth fifty blankets. He shook himself and combed the dry leaves out of his hair with his fingers. He marched forth into the comfortable morning sun, cold but confident, hungry but hopeful.

He had the world to himself, that early summer morning. The rustic road was soon joined by a canal, and he marched on by the water's edge. A solitary horse came plodding around a bend in the canal. Attached to his collar stretched a long rope, the further part of it dripping wet. Toad let the horse pass and stood waiting to see what its rope was tied to.

The horse was pulling a boat, and Toad watched as the barge slid up alongside him with a pleasant swirl of quiet water at its bow. Its lone occupant was a stout woman wearing a sunbonnet, one brawny arm laid along the tiller.

"A nice morning, ma'am!" she remarked to Toad.

"I daresay it is, ma'am," responded Toad politely, as he walked along the path. "I daresay it's a nice morning to them that's not in sore trouble like I am," Toad continued. "My married daughter wrote to me to come to her at once. So here I am, not knowing what may be happening. And I've lost all my money, and lost my way!"

"Where might your married daughter be living, ma'am?" asked the barge woman.

"She lives near to the river, ma'am," replied Toad. "Close to a fine house called Toad Hall. Perhaps you may have heard of it."

"Toad Hall, why I'm going that way myself," replied the barge woman. "You come along with me, and I'll give you a lift."

She steered the barge close to the bank, and a thankful Toad stepped lightly on board. "Toad's luck again!" he thought. "I always come out on top!"

"So, you're in the washing business, ma'am?" said the barge woman politely as they glided along. "And a very good business you've got, too."

"Finest business in the whole country," said Toad. "A real pleasure, I assure you."

"What a piece of luck meeting you!" said the barge woman thoughtfully. "A regular piece of good fortune for both of us!"

"Why, what do you mean?" asked the Toad nervously.

"Well, look at me, now," replied the barge woman. "*I* like washing, too, and whether I like it or not I have to do it all myself. There's a heap of things of mine that you'll find in a corner of the cabin. If you'll just take one or two and put them through the washtub as we go along, why it'll be a pleasure to you and a real help to me."

Toad was worried. He looked for an escape this way and that, but soon knew he had no choice. "I suppose any fool can wash," he thought.

He fetched the tub and soap from the cabin, selected a few pieces of clothing at random, and tried to remember what he had seen in casual glances through laundry windows.

A long hour of washing clothes passed, and every minute of it saw Toad getting angrier. He tried soaping, he tried scrubbing, he tried rinsing. His back ached badly, and he noticed that his paws were beginning to get crinkly. Now, Toad was very proud of his paws. He muttered under his breath words that should never pass the lips of washerwomen or Toads, and lost the soap for the fiftieth time. A burst of laughter made him look around. The barge woman was leaning back and laughing till the tears ran down her cheeks.

"I've been watching you all the time," she

gasped. "You've never washed so much as a dish-cloth in your life!"

Toad's temper, which had been simmering for some time now, fairly boiled over, and he lost all control of himself.

"You mean woman!" he shouted. "Don't you dare talk to me like that. I would have you know that I am a very well-known, distinguished Toad and I will not be laughed at by anyone!"

The woman moved nearer to him. "Why, so you are!" she cried. "Well, I never! A horrid, nasty, crawly Toad! And in my nice clean barge, too! Now, that is a thing I will *not* have."

One big arm shot out and caught Toad by a foreleg, while the other gripped him by a hind leg. Then the world turned suddenly upside down and Toad found himself flying through the air, revolving rapidly as he went.

The water, when he reached it with a loud splash, proved too cold for his taste. He rose to the surface spluttering, and the first thing he saw was the barge woman looking back at him and laughing. He vowed, as he coughed and choked, to get even with her. But the rapid water dragged him along with a force he could not stop. He was pulled straight into the river.

Toad rose to the surface and tried to grasp the reeds and rushes that grew along the water's edge, but the stream tore them out of his hands. But he soon saw that he was approaching a big, dark hole in the side of the riverbank, just above his head. As the stream raced him past, he reached up, caught hold of the edge of the hole, and held on. Slowly, and with difficulty, he drew himself out of the water, till at last he was able to rest his elbows on the edge of the hole. Toad's legs dangled over the edge and he felt the spray of the river rushing below him.

Toad stared ahead into the dark hole. Something small was moving in its depths, inching toward him. As it approached, a face gradually became clear, and it was a familiar face!

Brown and small, with whiskers.

Serious and round, with neat ears and silky hair.

It was Rat!

CHAPTER 16

Like Summer Storms
Came His Tears

⌒〜

The Rat put out a neat little paw, gripped Toad firmly by the neck, and gave a great hoist and a pull. The waterlogged Toad came up slowly but surely over the edge of the hole, till at last he stood safe and sound in the hall of Rat's underground home.

"O, Ratty!" he cried. "I've been through such times since I saw you last, I can't think! O, I *am* a smart Toad, and no mistake! Just hold on till I tell you—"

"Toad," said the Water Rat gravely, "you go off

upstairs at once, and take off that old cotton rag that looks as if might have belonged to some washerwoman. Clean yourself thoroughly and put on some of my clothes. I have never in my whole life seen a more shabby, disreputable object than you!"

Toad very quickly and humbly went upstairs. By the time he came down again, lunch was on the table, and Toad was very glad to see it. While they ate, Toad told Rat all his adventures, dwelling mainly on his own cleverness. But the more he talked and boasted, the more silent Rat became.

When at last Toad had talked himself to a standstill, Rat said, "Now, Toady, I don't want to give you pain after all you've been through, but don't you see what an awful fool you've been making of yourself?"

Toad heaved a great sigh and said very nicely, "Quite right, Ratty. Yes, I've always been a stuckup old fool; but now I'm going to be a good Toad, and not do it anymore. The fact is, while I was hanging on to the edge of the hole, I suddenly realized I've had enough of adventures for now. We'll have our coffee, and then I'm going to stroll down to Toad Hall."

"Stroll down to Toad Hall?" cried the Rat. "Do you mean to say you've heard nothing about the ferrets and stoats and weasels, and how they've taken over Toad Hall?"

Toad leaned his elbows on the table, his chin on his paws. A large tear welled up in each of his eyes, overflowed, and splashed on the table, plop! plop!

"Go on, Ratty," he murmured, "tell me everything."

"When you got into that trouble, it was a good deal talked about down here," continued the Rat. "The Wild Wood animals went about saying you would never come back again, never, never!"

Toad nodded, keeping silent.

"But Mole and Badger, they stuck by you, through thick and thin. They said that you would come back again, somehow. They arranged to move their things into Toad Hall and have it all ready for you when you turned up. But one dark night, a band of weasels, armed to the teeth, crept silently up to the front entrance. At the same time, a gang of desperate ferrets and stoats came around the back. The Mole and the Badger were sitting by the fire, suspecting nothing, when those bloodthirsty villains broke down the doors and rushed in on them from every side. They put up the best fight they could, but what was the use? The Wild Wooders outnumbered them and turned them out in the cold and wet. And they have been living at Toad Hall ever since, telling everybody that they've come to stay for good."

"O have they?" said Toad, getting up and grabbing a stick. "I'll soon see about that!"

"It's no good, Toad!" called the Rat after him.

"You'd better come back and sit down. You'll only get in trouble."

But the Toad was off, and there was no holding him back. He popped out of the hole and marched rapidly down the road, his stick over his shoulder. He was fuming and muttering to himself till he got near his front gate, when suddenly

there popped up a long, yellow ferret with a giant wooden club.

"Who comes there?" said the ferret sharply.

"Stuff and nonsense!" said the Toad very angrily. "What do you mean by talking like that to me?"

The ferret never said a word, but brought his club up to over his head. The Toad ducked flat in the road, and "whoosh!"

the swing of the club whistled over his head.

The startled Toad scrambled to his feet and scampered off down the road. As he ran, he heard the ferret laughing, and other horrid thin little laughs joining in.

He went back and told the Water Rat.

"What did I tell you?" said the Rat. "They've got guards all around and they're all armed. We can do nothing until we have seen the Mole and the Badger. Let's hear their latest news and take their advice in this difficult matter."

"Ah, yes, of course, the Mole and the Badger," said Toad lightly. "What's become of them, the dear fellows? I had forgotten all about them."

"Well may you ask!" said the Rat. "Those two poor, devoted animals have been camping out in the open outside Toad Hall, in every sort of weather, keeping a constant eye on the ferrets and stoats and weasels, and planning how to get your house back for you. You don't deserve to have such true, loyal friends, Toad. Someday, when it's too late, you'll be sorry you didn't value them more while you had them!"

"I'm an ungrateful beast, I know," sobbed Toad, shedding bitter tears. "Let me go out and find them, out into the cold, and share their hardships . . . Hold on a bit! Surely, I heard the clink of dishes on a tray! Supper's here at last! Come on, Ratty!"

The Rat remembered that poor Toad had been eating prison food, so he decided not to be angry over Toad's selfishness. Rat followed Toad to the table. They had just finished their meal when they heard a heavy knock on the door.

Toad was nervous, but the Rat went straight to the door and opened it. In walked Mr. Badger.

His shoes were covered in mud, and he was looking very rough. He came solemnly up to Toad, shook his paw, and said, "Welcome home, Toad! Alas, what am I saying? Home, indeed. This is a poor homecoming. Poor Toad!" Then he turned his back on him, sat down at the table, and helped himself to a large slice of pie.

Soon there came another knock, lighter this time. The Rat went to the door and ushered in Mole, very shabby and unwashed with bits of hay and straw sticking in his fur.

"Hooray! Here's old Toad!" cried the Mole, his face beaming. "We never dreamed you would turn up so soon! Why, you must have managed to escape, you smart, clever, intelligent Toad!"

The Rat, alarmed, pulled the Mole by the elbow, but it was already too late. Toad was puffing and swelling with pride already.

"Well, well," said the Mole, moving toward the supper table, "You talk while I eat. I haven't had a bite since breakfast! O my! O my!" And he sat down and helped himself to cold beef and pickles.

"Toad, do be quiet, please," said the Rat.

"Don't egg him on, Mole," said the Rat. "You know what he's like. But please tell us what the situation is at Toad Hall and what's to be done now that Toad is back at last."

"The situation is about as bad as it can be," replied the Mole grumpily. "And as for what's to be done, I have no idea! The Badger and I have been around and around the place by night and by day. There are always animals on the lookout, and when they see us—my! How they do laugh! That's what annoys me the most!"

"It's a very difficult situation," said the Rat. "But I see now what Toad really must do. He must . . ."

"No, he must not," shouted the Mole with a mouthful of food. "Nothing of the sort! What he must do . . ."

"Well, I won't do it, anyway," cried Toad, getting excited. "It's my house we're talking about and I know exactly what to do. I'm going to . . ."

They were all talking at once when a thin dry voice made itself heard, saying, "Be quiet at once, all of you!" Instantly everyone was silent.

It was the Badger, who, having finished his pie, had turned around in his chair and was looking at them very severely. He got up from his seat and stood before the fireplace, thinking deeply. At last he spoke.

"Toad!" he said sternly. "You bad, troublesome little animal! What do you think your father, my old friend, would have said if he had been here tonight, and had known of all your goings-on?"

Toad, who was on the sofa by this time with his legs up, rolled over on his face, shaking with shameful sobs.

"There, there!" went on the Badger more kindly. "Never mind. Stop crying. We're going to put this behind us and try to turn over a new leaf. But what Mole says is true. The ferrets and stoats and weasels are surrounding Toad Hall, and they make the best guards in the world."

"Then it's all over," sobbed the Toad into the sofa cushions.

"Come, cheery up, Toady!" said the Badger. "Now I'm going to tell you a great secret. There is an underground passage that leads from the riverbank, quite near here, right up into the middle of Toad Hall."

"O, nonsense, Badger," said Toad, rather rudely. "I know every inch of Toad Hall inside and out. Nothing of the sort, I do assure you!"

"My young friend," said the Badger severely, "your father, who was a worthy animal—a lot worthier than some I know—was a close friend of mine, and told me a great deal of things he wouldn't have dreamed of telling you. I've found out a thing or two lately," the Badger continued. "There's going to be a big party at Toad Hall tomorrow night. It's somebody's birthday—the

Chief Weasel's, I believe—and all of the weasels will be gathered in the dining hall, eating and drinking and carrying on. No weapons of any sort whatsoever!"

"But the guards will be posted as usual," remarked the Rat.

"Exactly," said the Badger. "That's my point. The weasels will trust their excellent guards. That's where the passage comes in. It leads right up under the butler's pantry, next to the dining hall!"

"Aha! That squeaky board in the butler's pantry!" said the Toad.

"We shall creep quietly out into the butler's pantry—" cried the Mole.

"—with our swords and sticks!" shouted the Rat.

"—and rush in upon them," said the Badger.

"—and whack 'em, and whack 'em, and whack 'em!" cried the Toad, running around the room, jumping all over the chairs.

"Very well then," said the Badger. "Our plan is settled. So, as it's getting very late, all of you go to bed at once. We will make all the necessary preparations tomorrow."

Toad slept till a late hour the next morning, and by the time he got down he found that the other animals had finished their breakfast some time before. The Mole had slipped off somewhere by himself, and the Badger sat in the armchair, reading the paper.

When the Toad had finished his breakfast, he picked up a stout stick and swung it wildly at imaginary animals. "I'll get them for stealing my house!" he cried. "I'll get them. I'll get them!"

Soon the Mole came tumbling into the room, looking very pleased with himself. "I've been bothering the stoats."

"I hope you've been very careful, Mole," said the Rat anxiously.

"I found that old washerwoman dress that Toad came home in yesterday, hanging before the fire," explained the Mole. "So I put it on, and the bonnet as well, and I went off to Toad Hall. The guards were there, of course. 'Good morning, gentlemen!' I said. 'Want any washing done today?'

"They looked at me very proud and said, 'Go away, washerwoman! We don't do any washing on duty.' 'Or any other time?' says I. Some of the Stoats turned quite pink, and the sergeant in charge said, 'Now run away! My good woman, run away.' 'Run away?' I said. 'It won't be *me* that'll be running away in a very short time.'"

"O, *Mole*, how could you?" said the Rat, dismayed.

The Badger put down his paper.

"I said, 'My daughter, she washes for Mr. Badger,'" continued the Mole, "'and I know what

I'm talking about. A hundred bloodthirsty badgers are going to attack Toad Hall this very night, by the field, with six boatloads of rats coming up the river, while a body of toads, known as the Death-or-Glory Toads, will storm the orchard.' I told them there won't be much left of them by the time they're done. Then I ran away, and they were all as nervous and flustered as could be, running all ways at once, and falling all over each other."

"O, you silly Mole!" cried Toad. "You've spoiled everything!"

"No, Toad," said the Badger, in his dry, quiet way, "Mole has managed excellently. Good Mole! Clever Mole!"

The Toad was wild with jealousy, especially as he couldn't make out for the life of him why Mole was so clever for giving away their plans. Fortunately for him, before he could show his temper, the bell rang for lunch.

CHAPTER 17

The Return of Ulysses

When it began to grow dark, the Badger took a lantern in one paw, grasped a stick with the other, and said, "Now then, follow me! Mole first, because I'm very pleased with him. Rat next, and Toad last. And look, Toady, don't you chatter as much as usual, or you'll be sent back!"

The Badger led them along the river a little way, and then suddenly swung himself over the edge into a hole in the riverbank, a little above the water. At last they were in the secret passage. The expedition had really begun!

It was cold, and dark, and damp, and low, and narrow. They groped and shuffled along, with their ears pricked up, till at last the Badger said, "We should be pretty nearly under the hall."

Sure enough, the passage began to slope upward. They groped onward a little farther, and then the noise broke out, very close above them. "Hoo-ray—hoo—ray—ray—ray!" they heard, and the stamping of little feet on the floor, and the pounding of little fists on the tables. "*What* a time they're having!" said the Badger. "Come on!" They hurried along the passage till it came to a full stop, where they found themselves standing under the trapdoor that led up into the butler's pantry.

Such a tremendous noise was going on in the banquet hall that there was little danger of being heard. The Badger said, "Now, boys, all together!" and the four of them put their shoulders to the trapdoor and heaved it open.

The noise as they came up from the passage

was simply deafening. At last, as the cheering and hammering subsided, a voice could be made out saying, "Well, I do not propose to keep you much longer—(great applause)—but before I take my seat, I should like to say one word about our kind host, Mr. Toad. We all know Toad!—(great laughter)—*Good* Toad, *modest* Toad, *honest* Toad!" (shrieks of merriment).

"Let me get him!" muttered Toad, grinding his teeth.

"Hold on a minute!" said the Badger, holding Toad back with difficulty. "Get ready, all of you!"

The Badger drew himself up, took a firm grip of his stick with both paws, glanced around at his friends, and cried—

"The hour is come! Follow me!"

The door flung wide open.

My!

What a squealing and a squeaking and a screeching filled the air!

The affair was soon over. Up and down the length of the hall strode the four comrades, whacking with their sticks and sending their surprised enemies scattering. In five minutes the room was clear. Through the broken windows the shrieks of fleeing weasels could be heard. The Badger, resting on his stick, wiped his brow.

"Mole," he said, "you are the best of fellows! Just go and make sure those guards are running away, too. Thanks to you, they were expecting an attack from outside, but not from below. We won't have much trouble from *them*!"

The Mole vanished through a window, and Badger asked the others to set a table on its legs again. "I want some food, I do," he said. "Stir your stumps, Toad, and look lively! We've got your house back for you and you haven't offered us so much as a sandwich."

Toad felt rather hurt that the Badger didn't praise him, as he had praised Mole. But he bustled about, and so did the Rat, and soon they found some jelly in a glass dish, and a cold chicken, and quite a bit of lobster salad, and a great quantity of cheese, butter, and celery. They were just about to sit down when the Mole clambered in through the window, chuckling.

"It's all over," he reported. "As soon as the guards heard the shrieks and the yells inside the hall, some of them threw down their weapons and fled. The others stood fast for a bit, but when the weasels came rushing out, they all disappeared."

"Excellent and deserving animal!" said the Badger.

Then the Mole pulled his chair up to the table and pitched into the cold chicken. Toad, like the gentleman he was, put all his jealousy aside and said heartily, "Thank you kindly, dear Mole, for all of your pains this evening, and especially for your cleverness this morning!" The Badger was pleased at that and added, "Well spoken, my brave Toad!"

They finished their supper in great joy and contentment and soon retired to sleep, between clean sheets, in soft beds, safe in Toad's ancestral home.

After this excitement, the four animals continued to lead their lives in great happiness and ease, undisturbed by further uprisings or invasions. Toad, after due consultation with his friends, selected a handsome gold chain and locket set with pearls, which he sent to the jailer's daughter with a letter of thanks for helping him escape. Even the Badger admitted that Toad had become modest, grateful, and appreciative. The engine driver, in turn, was properly thanked for his pains and troubles. And, under severe pressure from Badger, even the barge woman was found and thanked, though Toad kicked terribly at this.

Sometimes, in the course of long summer evenings, the friends would take a stroll together in the Wild Wood, now successfully tamed so far as they were concerned. It was pleasing to see how respectfully they were greeted by its inhabitants, and how the mother weasels would bring their young ones to the mouths of their holes, and say, pointing, "Look, baby! There goes the great Mr. Toad! And that's the gallant Water Rat! And yonder comes the famous Mr. Mole, of whom you have heard your father tell!" But when their children were quite beyond control, they would quiet them by telling how, if they didn't hush up, the terrible gray Badger would come and scold them. This was not true in the slightest. Badger, though he cared very little about society, was rather fond of children. But it never failed to have its full effect.

What Do *You* Think?
Questions for Discussion

⌒∽

Have you ever been around a toddler who keeps asking the question "Why?" Does your teacher call on you in class with questions from your homework? Do your parents ask you questions about your day at the dinner table? We are always surrounded by questions that need a specific response. But is it possible to have a question with no right answer?

The following questions are about the book you just read. But this is not a quiz! They are designed to help you look at the people, places, and events in the story from different angles. These questions do not have specific answers. Instead, they might make you think of the story in a completely new way.

Think carefully about each question and enjoy discovering more about this classic story.

1. All of the main characters in this book are animals. Why do you think this is? If you could be any kind of animal, what would you choose to be?

2. Toad changes his mind about the best way to travel every few days. Why do you think the car continues to fascinate him? What kinds of transportation have you used? Which was your favorite?

3. The Wild Wood seems friendly when the Mole first enters it, but he soon grows scared of everything around him. Do you think the woods are actually dangerous, or is it just his imagination? What's the scariest place you've ever been?

4. The Badger seems very grumpy when the Rat and the Mole first arrive at his house, but his attitude quickly changes when he realizes who is at the door. Why do you suppose this is? Do you have any friends that you're always happy to see?

5. How does the Mole react when he smells his home? Why do you suppose this happens? Have you ever been homesick?

6. Toad says, "A worthy fellow, Ratty, with many good qualities, but very little intelligence." Do you agree? What do you think the Rat's best quality is? What's your best quality?

7. At one point in the story, the Rat and the Mole learn that the Otter's son is lost. How do you suppose this made the Otter feel? Have you ever been lost? How did you find your way home again?

8. Everyone Toad meets seems to want to help him. Why do you think this is? Have you ever known anyone like Toad?

9. When the Rat meets the seafaring rat, he is struck by an overwhelming desire to travel with him. Have you ever traveled? Where would you most like to visit?

10. Why does the Badger say that the Mole "managed excellently" by telling the stoats and weasels about the coming attack? Do you think the Mole did this on purpose, or did he accidentally do a good thing? Have you ever tricked someone to your advantage?

Afterword
by Arthur Pober, EdD

◌

First impressions are important.

Whether we are meeting new people, going to new places, or picking up a book unknown to us, first impressions count for a lot. They can lead to warm, lasting memories or can make us shy away from any future encounters.

Can you recall your own first impressions and earliest memories of reading the classics?

Do you remember wading through pages and pages of text to prepare for an exam? Or were you the child who hid under the blanket to read with a flashlight, joining forces with Robin Hood to save Maid Marian? Do you remember only how long it took you to read a lengthy novel such as *Little Women*? Or did you become best friends with the March sisters?

Even for a gifted young reader, getting through long chapters with dense language can easily become overwhelming and can obscure the richness of the story and its characters. Reading an abridged, newly crafted version of a classic novel can be the gentle introduction a child needs to explore the characters and storyline without the frustration of difficult vocabulary and complex themes.

Reading an abridged version of a classic novel gives the young reader a sense of independence and the satisfaction of finishing a "grown-up" book. And when a child is engaged with and inspired by a classic story, the tone is set for further exploration of the story's themes, characters, history, and details. As a child's reading skills advance, the desire to tackle the original, unabridged version of the story will naturally emerge.

If made accessible to young readers, these stories can become invaluable tools for understanding themselves in the context of their families and social environments. This is why the Classic Starts series includes questions that stimulate discussion regarding the impact and social relevance of the characters and stories today. These questions can foster lively conversations between children and their parents or teachers. When we look at the issues, values, and standards of past times in terms of how we live now, we can appreciate literature's classic tales in a very personal and engaging way.

Share your love of reading the classics with a young child, and introduce an imaginary world real enough to last a lifetime.

Dr. Arthur Pober, EdD

Dr. Arthur Pober has spent more than twenty years in the fields of early childhood and gifted education. He is the former principal of one of the world's oldest laboratory schools for gifted youngsters, Hunter College Elementary School, and former Director of Magnet Schools for the Gifted and Talented for more than 25,000 youngsters in New York City.

Dr. Pober is a recognized authority in the areas of media and child protection and is currently the U.S. representative to the European Institute for the Media and European Advertising Standards Alliance.

Explore these wonderful stories in our
Classic Starts™ library.